This book
belongs to:

_____

MESSAGE TO PARENTS

This book is perfect for parents and children to read aloud together. First read the story to your child. When you read it again run your finger under each line, stopping at each picture for your child to "read." Help your child to figure out the picture. If your child makes a mistake, be encouraging as you say the right word. Point out the written word beneath each picture in the margin on the page. Soon your child will be "reading" aloud with you, and at the same time learning the symbols that stand for words.

Copyright © 1988 Checkerboard Press, a division of Macmillan, Inc. All rights reserved.
Printed in U.S.A. ISBN: 002-898132-4 Library of Congress Catalog Card Number: 88-25703
READ ALONG WITH ME books are conceived by Deborah Shine.

CHECKERBOARD PRESS, READ ALONG WITH ME, and their respective logos are trademarks of Macmillan, Inc.

0 9 8 7 6 5 4 3 2

The Little Red Hen

A Read Along With Me Book

Retold by **Cindy West**

Illustrated by **Olivia Cole**

CHECKERBOARD PRESS
NEW YORK

hen

chicks

house

duck

cat

pig

Once upon a time, there was a little red . She and her tiny little shared a rickety old with a and a and a fat pink .

The little red  worked hard all the time, taking care of the 🏠 and the 🏡 . But the other animals didn't do a thing. They were very lazy!

yard

pig

duck

cat

The pink 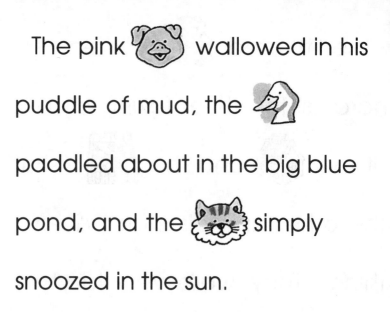 wallowed in his puddle of mud, the 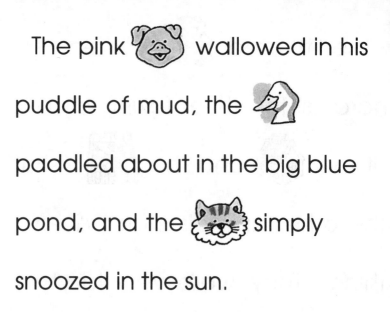 paddled about in the big blue pond, and the 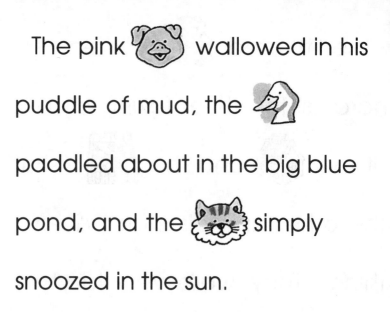 simply snoozed in the sun.

One spring day, when she was

cleaning the yard, the little red  found a packet of .

"How lucky we are," said the little red . "Who will help me plant these wonderful ?"

hen

seeds

pig

duck

cat

hen

"Not I," grunted the ,

sinking deeper into his mud.

"Not I," quacked the  ,

carefully preening her feathers.

"Not I," yawned the ,

going back to sleep.

"I will," said the little red .

So she raked the soil, and

pulled out the weeds, and

planted all the  in a neat

seeds

little row.

Every day, she carefully

watered the  and pulled

out all the weeds.

wheat

hen

As spring turned to summer, the seeds sprouted green shoots. Then the shoots grew into golden , rising taller and taller.

Finally the was ready to harvest. "Who will pick this ?" asked the little red .

"Not I," squealed the  .

"Not I," quacked the .

"Not I," yawned the .

"Then I will," said the little red

. And she picked all the

 in the hot, hot sun.

pig

duck

cat

tree

hen

wheat

pig

duck

cat

After a brief rest under a , the little red asked, "Who will take this to the mill?"

"Not I," squealed the .

"Not I," quacked the .

"Not I," yawned the .

"Then I will," said the little red . So she put on her , tucked her  into her pocket, and walked down the  to the mill.

hat

chicks

road

bag

wheat

hen

chicks

house

The miller took her of 🌾

and ground it into flour.

"Thank you!" said the little red

 , and she and her 🐥

walked back to their .

When she got home, the little

red  rested awhile in her

rocking . Then she asked,

"Who will bake some ?"

"Not I," squealed the .

"Not I," quacked the .

"Not I," yawned the .

chair

bread

pig

duck

cat

hen

pan

oven

"I will," sighed the little red .

So she spooned in the flour,

mixed in the yeast, and poured in

the milk. With all her strength, she

kneaded and kneaded the

dough. She put the dough in a

sturdy  and placed the

in the .

Then she sat and waited for the
 to bake.

After a while, a sweet smell
filled the  and floated out
the .

The and the and
the sat up and sniffed.
They raced to the .

bread

house

door

pig

duck

cat

hen

bread

pig

There they saw the little red holding a fine loaf of fresh warm  .

"I wonder," asked the little red very softly, "who is going to eat this  ?"

"I will!" laughed the , licking his lips.

"I will!" quacked the ,

flapping her wings.

"I will!" purred the ,

curling his tail.

"No you won't! We will!" said

the little red . "My

and I!"

And she and her sat

down at the and ate up

every last crumb!

duck

cat

chicks

table